JOAN AIKEN, the daughter of the American poet and novelist Conrad Aiken, was an immensely popular and prolific author who wrote over a hundred novels for adults and children. The creator of the stories about Arabel and her pet raven Mortimer, originally written for the BBC's Jackanory series and which have been televised on the BBC, she also wrote wonderful, quirky novels, full of humour and the unexpected. *The Wolves of Willoughby Chase* won the 1964 Lewis Carroll Shelf Award and was made into a film. Joan Aiken was awarded an MBE for her services to children's literature in 1999. She died in 2004.

QUENTIN BLAKE was born in 1932. His first illustrated children's book appeared in 1960, and since then he has worked on over 300, collaborating, among many other writers, with Russell Hoban, Michael Rosen, John Yeoman and, most famously, Roald Dahl. He is also known for his own picture books such as *Clown* and *Zagazoo*, and his illustrations to classics such as *Don Quixote* and *Candide*. In 1999 he was appointed first Children's Laureate. He was knighted in 2013 for services to illustration, and he is also a chevalier of the Légion d'Honneur.

THE SPIRAL STAIR

Joan Aiken
illustrated by
Quentin Blake

Frances Lincoln
Children's Books

First published in Great Britain in 1979
by the British Broadcasting Corporation
35 Marylebone High Street, London W1M 4AA

This edition published in 2015 by
Frances Lincoln Children's Books,
74-77 White Lion Street, London N1 9PF
www.franceslincoln.com

ISBN: 978-1-84780-694-9

A CIP catalogue record for this book
is available from the British Library

Printed and bound by CPI Group (UK) Ltd,
Croydon, CR0 4YY

1 3 5 7 9 8 6 4 2

Chapter One

"Excuse me. Are you two gentlemen going as far as Foxwell?" Mrs Jones inquired nervously, having opened the railway carriage door and poked her head through. The hand that was not holding the door-handle clasped the wrist of Mrs Jones's daughter Arabel, who was carrying a large canvas bag.

Mrs Jones had been opening doors and asking this question all the way along the train, when she thought the occupants of the carriage looked respectable. Some of them did not. Some weren't going as far as Foxwell.

But the two men in this carriage looked *very* respectable. Both had bowler hats. One was small and stout, one was large and pale. Their brief-cases were in the rack, and they were talking to one another in low, confidential, businesslike voices.

Now they stopped and looked at Mrs Jones as if they were rather put out at being interrupted. But one of them – the small fat one – said: "Yes, madam. We are getting out *at* Foxwell, as it happens."

The other man, the large pale one, frowned, as if he wished his friend had not been so helpful.

"Oh, are you, that's ever such a relief then," cried Mrs Jones, "for you look like nice reliable gentlemen and I'm sure you won't mind seeing that my little girl, that's Arabel here, gets out at Foxwell where her uncle Urk will be meeting her and I know it looks ever so peculiar my not going with her myself, but I have to hurry back to Rumbury Hospital where my hubby Mr Jones is having his various veins seen to and he likes me to visit him all the visiting hours and I couldn't leave poor little Arabel alone at home every day, let alone Mortimer, and my sister Brenda isn't a *bit* keen to have them, but luckily my hubby's brother Urk lives in the country and said he would oblige, leastways it was his wife Effie that wrote but Ben said Urk would know how to manage Mortimer on account of him being used to all kinds of wild –"

Luckily at this moment the guard blew a shrill blast on his whistle, for the two men were beginning to look even more impatient, so Mrs Jones hastily bundled Arabel into the railway carriage and dumped her suitcase on the seat beside her.

"Now you'll be ever such a good girl won't you dearie, and Mortimer too if he *can*, and take care among all those megadilloes and jumbos and do what Aunt Effie says – and we'll be down to fetch you on Friday fortnight –"

Here the guard interrupted Mrs Jones again by slamming the carriage door, so Mrs Jones blew kisses through the window as the train pulled away. One of the bowler-hatted men – the short fat one – got up and put Arabel's case in the rack where she couldn't reach it to get out her picture book. He would have done the same with the canvas bag she was carrying, but she clutched that tightly on her lap, so he sat down again.

The two men then took their hats off, laid them on the seat, settled themselves comfortably, and went on with their conversation, taking no notice whatever of Arabel, who was very small and fair-haired, and who sat very quietly in her corner.

After a minute or two she opened the canvas bag, out of which clambered a very large untidy black bird – almost as big as Arabel herself – who first put himself to rights with his beak, then stood tip-claw on Arabel's lap and stared out of the window at the suburbs of London rushing past.

He had never been in a train before, and was

so astonished at what he saw that he exclaimed
"*Nevermore!*" in a loud, hoarse, rasping voice
which had the effect of spinning round the heads
of the two men as if they had been jerked by wires.
They both stared very hard at Arabel and her pet.

"What kind of a bird is that?" asked one of
them, the large pale one.

"He's a raven," said Arabel, "and his name's
Mortimer."

"Oh!" said the pale man, losing interest.
"Quite a *common* bird."

"Mortimer's not a bit common," said Arabel,
offended.

"Well, I hope he behaves himself on this train," said the pale man, and then the two men went back to their conversation.

Mortimer, meanwhile, looked up and saw Arabel's suitcase in the rack above his head. Immediately he saw it he wanted to get up there too. But Arabel could not reach the rack, and Mortimer was not prepared to fly up. He disliked flying, and very rarely did so, if he could find somebody to lift him. He now said "Kaark," in a loud, frustrated tone.

"Excuse me," said Arabel very politely to the two men, "could you please put my raven up in the rack?"

This time, both men looked decidedly irritable at being interrupted.

"Certainly not," said the large pale one.

"Rack ain't the place for birds," said the short fat one. "No knowing *what* he might not get up to there."

"By rights he ought to be in the guard's van," said the first. "Any more bother from you and we'll call the guard to take him away."

They both stared hard and angrily at Arabel and Mortimer, and then began talking to one another again.

"We'd better hire a truck in Ditchingham – Fred will be there with the supplies, he can do it – have the truck waiting at Bradpole crossroads – you carry the tranquillisers, I'll have the nets – twenty ampoules ought to be enough, and a hundred yards of netting –"

"Don't forget the foam rubber –"

"Nevermore," grumbled Mortimer to himself, very annoyed at not getting what he wanted immediately he wanted it.

"Look at the sheep and the dear little lambs in that field, Mortimer," said Arabel, for the train had now left London and was running through green country. But Mortimer was not in the least interested in dear little lambs. While Arabel was watching them, he very quietly and neatly hacked one of the men's bowler hats into three pieces with his huge beak, and then swallowed the bits

in three gulps. Neither of the men noticed what he had done. They were deep in plans.

"*You* take care of the ostriches – mind, they kick – and *I'll* look after the zebras."

"They kick too."

"Just have to be nippy with the tranquilliser, that's all."

Mortimer, coming to the conclusion that nobody was going to help him, hoisted himself up into the rack with one strong shove-off and two flaps. The men were so absorbed in their plans that they did not notice this either.

"Here's a map of the area – the truck had better park here – by the ostrich enclosure –"

Mortimer, up above them, suddenly did his celebrated imitation of the sound of a milk-float rattling along a cobbled street. "Clinketty-clang, clang, clink, clanketty clank."

Both men glanced about them in a puzzled manner.

"Funny," said the short fat man, "could have sworn I heard a milk cart."

"Don't be daft," said the large pale one. "How could you hear a *milk-cart* in a *train*? Now – we have to think how to get rid of the watchman –"

Mortimer now silently worked his way along the rack until he was over the men's heads. He wanted to have a look at their luggage. From one of the two flat black cases there stuck out a small thread of white down. Mortimer took a quiet pull at this. Out came a straggly piece of ostrich feather. Mortimer studied the bit of plume for a long time, sniffed at it, listened to it, and finally poked it under his wing. Presently, forgetting about it, he hung upside down from the rack, swaying to and fro with the motion of the train, and breathing deeply with pleasure.

"Please take care, Mortimer," said Arabel softly.

Mortimer gave her a very carefree look. Then, showing off, he let go with one claw. However at that moment the train went over a set of points – kerblunk – and Mortimer's hold became detached. He fell, heavily.

By great good luck Arabel, who was anxiously watching, saw Mortimer let go, and so she was able, holding wide the two handles of the canvas bag, to catch him – he went into the bag head-first.

The ostrich-plume drifted to the floor.

The two men, busy with their plans, noticed nothing of this.

The fat one was saying, "The giraffes are the most important. Reckon we should pack them in first, they take up most room?"

"Nah, can't. Giraffes have to be *un*loaded first. They're wanted by a customer in Woking."

"Why the blazes should somebody want *giraffes* in *Woking*?"

"How should *I* know? Not our business, anyway."

Mortimer poked his head out of the canvas bag. He was very annoyed at his mortifying fall, and ready to make trouble, if possible. His eye lit on the second bowler hat.

Fortunately at this moment the train began to slow down.

Nearly at Foxwell now, little girl," said the fat man. He took down Arabel's case and put it by her on the seat.

"You being met here?" he said.

"Yes," said Arabel. "My Uncle Urk is meeting me. He is –" But the two men weren't paying any attention to her. The large one was looking for his hat. "Funny, I put it just here. Where the devil can it have got to?"

"Oh dear," said Arabel politely, when no hat

could be found. "I'm afraid my raven may have eaten it. He *does* eat things sometimes."

"Rubbish," said the hatless man.

"Don't be silly," said the fat man.

Now the train came to a stop, and Arabel, through the window, saw her Uncle Urk on the platform. She waved to him and he came and opened the door.

"There you are, then," he said. "Enjoy your trip? This all your luggage?"

Uncle Urk was brown and wrinkled, with a lot of bristly grey hair. There were bits of straw clinging to his clothes.

"Yes, thank you, Uncle Urk."

"That's right." He took Arabel's case, and she carried the bag with Mortimer in it. "Goodbye," she called to the two men, but they were still busy hunting for the lost hat.

"Look at this!" the pale one said angrily to the thin one, finding the bit of ostrich-plume on the floor. "You careless fool!" He quickly picked up the feather and stuck it in his pocket.

Uncle Urk dropped Arabel's case in the back of his pick-up truck and settled her and Mortimer in the front seat.

"Well? You excited at the thought of staying in a zoo?" he inquired.

"Yes, thank you," said Arabel. "Mortimer is too, aren't you, Mortimer?"

"Kaaark," said Mortimer.

Chapter Two

"Do you keep *every* kind of animal in your zoo, Uncle Urk?" Arabel asked.

"It ain't my zoo really, Arabel, you know. I'm just the head warden, and your Aunt Effie runs the cafeteria," said Uncle Urk. "The zoo belongs to Lord Donisthorpe."

"Does he have lions and tigers?"

"No, he hasn't got any of those. He likes grass-eating animals mostly – wildebeests and zebras and giraffes. And birds and snakes. And he's got porcupines and a hippopotamus and a baby elephant. I expect you'll enjoy giving the baby elephant doughnuts."

"I thought they liked buns best?" said Arabel.

"Lord Donisthorpe has invented a doughnut-making machine," said her uncle. "It uses whole-wheat flour and sunflower oil and honey, so the doughnuts it makes are very good for the animals. And so they blooming well oughter be at thirty pence apiece," he muttered to himself. "Cor! Did you ever? Six bob for a perishing doughnut!"

His truck at that moment passed between gates in a high wire-mesh fence. Arabel noticed a sign that said, "Caution, zebra crossing."

Ahead of them lay a ruined-looking castle, inside a moat, and a lot of wooden and stone buildings and haystacks. But Uncle Urk pulled up in front of a small white house with a neat garden around it. "Here's your Aunt Effie and Chris Cross," he said.

Chris was a boy who used to live next door to Arabel's family in Rumbury Town, London. But he had come down to work in Lord Donisthorpe's zoo as a holiday job last summer, and liked it so much that he stayed on.

Aunt Effie was thin-faced and fuzzy-haired; her eyes were pale-blue but sharp. Nearly all her remarks about people began with the words, "You can't blame them –" which really meant that she *did* blame them, very much. "You can't blame the kids who drop their ice-lolly papers; they've never learned no better, nasty little things. You can't blame murderers, it's their nature; what I say is, they ought to make them into pet-food. You can't blame your Uncle Urk for being such a muddler; he was born that way."

Now Aunt Effie's pale-blue eyes snapped as she looked at Mortimer clambering out of his canvas bag, and she said, "Well, I s'pose you can't blame Martha for sending that monster down with Arabel. *I* wouldn't leave him alone in the house myself, wouldn't keep him a day, but so long as he stays in *my* house, he stops inside the meat-safe, that's the place for him!"

She fetched a galvanised zinc cupboard with a perforated door into the front hall and said to Arabel, "Put the bird in there!"

"Oh, *please* not, Aunt Effie," said Arabel, horrified. "Mortimer would hate that, he really would! He's used to being out. I'll keep an eye on him, I promise."

"Well: the very first thing he pokes or breaks with that great beak of his," said Aunt Effie, "into the meat-safe he goes!"

Mortimer looked very subdued. He sat beside Arabel at tea, keeping quite quiet, but Arabel

managed to cheer him up by slipping pieces
of Aunt Effie's lardy-cake to him. It was very
delicious – chewy and crunchy, with pieces of
buttery toffee-like sugar in among the dough, and
a lot of currants.

After tea, Aunt Effie had to go back to manage
the cafeteria. Chris said, "I'm going to feed the
giraffes, so I'll show Arabel over the zoo, a bit,
shall I?"

"Mind she's not a nuisance," said Aunt Effie.

Uncle Urk, who was also going to feed animals, said he would probably meet them near the camel-house.

Lord Donisthorpe's zoo was in the large park which lay all round his castle. Lord Donisthorpe lived in the castle, which was in bad repair. The animals mostly lived in the open air, roaming about eating the grass. They had wooden huts and stone houses for cold weather, or to sleep in. Builders were putting up more of these. They were also at work building an enormously high stone wall to replace the wire-mesh fence round the park.

"Is that to stop the animals escaping?" asked Arabel.

"No, they don't want to escape. They like it here," said Chris. "It's to stop thieves getting in. There have been a lot of robberies from zoos lately. When this one was smaller, Lord Donisthorpe just used to leave Noah the boa loose at night, and he took care of any thieves that got in. But now the zoo's getting so big there's too much ground to cover – Noah can't be everywhere at once."

Just at that moment Mortimer's eye was

attracted by a beautiful stretch of smooth wet cement which the builders had just laid. It was going to be the floor of the new porcupine palace. Quick as lightning Mortimer flopped off Arabel's shoulder and walked across the cement, leaving a trail of deeply indented bird-prints.

"Gerroff there, you black buzzard!" shouted a workman, and he threw a trowel at Mortimer, who, startled, flew up into the nearest dark hole he could find. This happened to be the mouth of the cement-mixer, which was turning round and round.

"Oh, please, quick, stop the mixer!" cried Arabel. "Please get him out!"

A confused sight of feet and tail-feathers could be seen sticking out of the mixer. The man who was running it stopped the engine that turned the hopper, and tipped it so that it pointed downwards. Out came a great slop of half-mixed cement, and Mortimer, so coated over that nothing could be seen of him but his feet and black feathery trousers.

"We'd best pour a bucket of water over him before it sets," said Chris, and did so. "Lucky your Aunt Effie wasn't around when *that* happened,"

he added, as Mortimer, croaking and gasping, re-
appeared from under the cement. "That'd be
quite enough to get him shut up in the meat-safe."

"Mortimer, you *must* be *careful* here," said
Arabel anxiously.

Mortimer might have been put out by his
mishap with the cement-mixer – things like that
often made him very bad-tempered – but luckily
his attention was distracted just then by the sight
of a herd of zebra, all black-and-white stripes.

"Nevermore!" he said, utterly amazed, staring with all his might as the zebra strolled across the road.

Then they passed a group of ostriches, who looked very vague and absent-minded, as ostriches do, and were preening themselves in a patch of sand. When he was close by them, Mortimer did his celebrated imitation of an ambulance rushing past with bell clanging and siren wailing.

All the ostriches immediately stuck their heads in the sand.

"You better tell Mortimer not to make that noise in your Aunt Effie's house," said Chris. "Your Aunt Effie doesn't like noise."

Now they passed a cage which had an enormous, sleepy-looking, greedy-looking snake inside it. "That's Noah the boa," said Chris. "He's very fond of doughnuts. Want to give him one?"

Arabel did not much care for the look of Noah the boa, but she did want to see how the doughnut machine worked. There was one near Noah's cage. It had a glass panel in front, and a slot for putting in a ten-penny piece.

"The public have to put in three coins to get a doughnut," said Chris, "but luckily there's a lever behind that only zoo staff know about, so we can get ours for one. You have to put in one ten-penny piece to get it started; after that you keep pulling the lever."

He dropped a coin in the slot. Instantly an uncooked doughnut rolled down a chute into a pan of boiling oil behind the glass panel, and began to fry. After a minute or two, a wire hook fished it out of the oil and held it up to dry.

"Now, if you were a member of the public, you'd have to put in another coin to get it sugared," said Chris. "But as we're zoo staff we can pull the lever." He did so, and a puffer blew a cloud of honey-crystals all over the doughnut so that it became fuzzed with white.

"Now what happens?" said Arabel.

"Now if you were a member of the public you'd have to put in a third coin to get it out," said Chris. He pulled the lever again. The hook let go of the doughnut, which rolled down another chute and was delivered into a crinkled paper cup-cake case.

Mortimer, who had been watching all this with extreme interest, took a step forward along Arabel's

arm. But Noah the boa had also been watching –
at the first clank of the coin in the machine all his
sleepiness had left him – and as Arabel took the
doughnut from the paper cup he opened his
mouth so wide that his jaws were in a straight
line up and down. Arabel rather timidly tossed in
the doughnut, and Noah's jaws shut with a snap.

"His jaws are hinged so that he can swallow
an animal as big as a pig if he wants to," said
Chris. "But he prefers doughnuts; they are his
favourite food."

"How do you know?" said Arabel. "He doesn't *look* pleased."

"Things he doesn't like he spits out," said Chris.

'Kaaark," said Mortimer, in a gloomy aggrieved tone.

"All right, Mortimer," said Arabel. "Ma gave me a ten-pee piece, so I'll do a doughnut for you now, if Chris doesn't mind pulling the levers."

She dropped in her coin, and another raw doughnut slid into the boiling oil.

Mortimer's eyes shone at the sight, and he began to jump up and down on Arabel's shoulder.

When the doughnut was cooked and sugared, Chris pulled the lever to release it into the paper cup.

"Suppose a person only had two ten-pee pieces?" said Arabel.

"Then they better not start, or they'd have to go off and leave the doughnut waiting there for the next customer," said Chris. "But that doesn't often happen. Who'd be such a mug as to leave twenty-pee's worth of doughnut for someone else to pick up for only ten-pee?

Just as Mortimer's doughnut came out, something unfortunate happened. A small head on a very long spotted neck came gently over Arabel's shoulder and nibbled up the doughnut so fast and neatly and quietly that for a moment Mortimer could not believe that it had gone. Then he let out a fearful wail of dismay.

"Nevermore!"

"Oh dear," said Chris. "That's Derek. These giraffes are just mad about doughnuts. If they see anybody near the machine they come crowding round."

Arabel turned, and, sure enough, three giraffes had come silently up behind them, and were standing in a ring, evidently hoping that more doughnuts were going to be served.

"Their names are Wendy, Elsie, and Derek," Chris said.

"I'm *dreadfully* sorry, Mortimer," Arabel said. "I haven't any more money."

Neither had Chris.

Mortimer made not the least attempt to conceal his disappointment and indignation. He jumped up and down, he screamed terrible words at the giraffes, who looked at him calmly and affably.

"What the dickens is the matter with that bird?" asked Uncle Urk, passing by with a bucket of wildebeest food.

"Derek ate his doughnut," said Chris.

"Well for the land's sake, give him another," said Uncle Urk, who was very goodnatured. "Here's ten-pee."

"Oh, thank you, Uncle Urk," said Arabel. This time she pulled the levers, for Chris had to get on with his evening jobs.

When the doughnut came down the chute, Mortimer, who had been watching like a sprinter waiting for the tape to go down, lunged in and grabbed it just before Wendy could bend her long neck down.

He was so pleased with himself at having got in ahead of Wendy that, contrary to his usual habit, he rose up in the air, holding the doughnut in his beak, and flew vengefully and provokingly round and round the high heads of the giraffes.

"Mortimer, stop it! That isn't kind," said Arabel. "Just eat your doughnut and don't tease."

Mortimer took no notice. He swooped between Derek and Wendy, who banged their heads together as they both tried to snatch the doughnut. This amused Mortimer so much that by mistake he let go of the doughnut – which fell to the ground and was seized and – swallowed by Elsie.

Mortimer drew a great breath of fury; all his feathers puffed out like a fancy chrysanthemum.

However, Arabel grabbed him and said: "That just serves you right, Mortimer. I haven't any more money, so you'll have to go without a doughnut now. Come along, we'd better go and see some more of Uncle Urk's zoo."

She walked on, but Mortimer was very displeased indeed, and kept looking back at the giraffes and muttering, "Nevermore, nevermore, nevermore," under his breath.

Then they met Lord Donisthorpe, the owner of the zoo. He was a tall, straggly man, who looked not unlike his own giraffes and ostriches, except that he was not spotty, and had no tail feathers. He had a very long neck, and untidy white hair, and a vague expression.

"Ah, yes," he said, observing Arabel over the tops of his glasses, which were shaped like segments of orange. "You must be Mr Jones's niece, come to stay. I hope you are enjoying your visit. But your raven seems out of spirits."

This was an understatement. Mortimer was now shrieking "Nevermore!" at the top of his lungs, and spinning himself round and round on one leg.

"One of the giraffes ate his doughnut," Arabel explained.

"Perhaps he would like an ice-cream in the cafeteria?" inquired Lord Donisthorpe. "Perhaps you would too? They are very good. We make our own."

"Thank you, we should both like that very much," said Arabel politely.

On the way to the cafeteria they passed an immensely tall building made of wood and glass. "That is my new giraffe house," said Lord Donisthorpe.

At the word *giraffe* Mortimer looked ready to bash anyone who came near him.

The giraffe house was built to suit the shapes of the giraffes, with high windows, so that they could see out, and a spiral staircase in the middle, leading to a circular gallery, so that visitors could climb up and be on a level with the giraffes' faces. The walls of the building were not finished yet; one side was open. Mortimer looked very sharply at the spiral stair, and Arabel kept a firm hold of his leg, for he had been known to eat stairs on several occasions in the past. However these stairs

were made of ornamental ironwork, and it
seemed likely that even Mortimer would find
them tough.

"Come on, Mortimer, Lord Donisthorpe's
going to buy you an ice-cream," Arabel said.

"Kaaark," said Mortimer doubtfully.

The cafeteria, just beyond the giraffe house,
had another doughnut machine by its door.

Mortimer stared at this very hard as they walked by, but Lord Donisthorpe led the way into the cafeteria itself, which had red tables and shiny metal chairs and a counter with orange and lemon and coffee machines and piles of things to eat. Aunt Effie was at the counter, standing behind a glass case filled with cream-cheese patties and toffee-covered carrots on sticks.

"We make our own toffee-carrots," said Lord Donisthorpe. "They are very wholesome indeed. And we have three different flavours of home-made ice-cream, dandelion, blackcurrant, and quince. Which would you prefer?"

Arabel chose the quince, which was a beautiful orange-red colour; Mortimer indicated that he would like the dandelion, which was bright yellow.

Aunt Effie gave them a disapproving look. "*I* don't know; eating again, only half an hour after they had their tea," she muttered, scooping out the ice-cream and ramming it into cornets. "But I s'pose you can't blame them, brought up by that empty-headed Martha."

While she was serving out the ice-cream, Mortimer noticed that an empty tray had been

left at one end of the cafeteria rail.

Flopping off Arabel's shoulder on to the tray
he gave himself a powerful push-off with his tail
and shot along the rail past the counter as if he
had been on a toboggan, shouting "Nevermore!"
and spreading his wings out wide. His left-hand
wing knocked a whole row of cream-cheese
patties into the blackcurrant ice-cream bin.

Aunt Effie let out a shriek of rage. "How
Martha can stand that Fiend of a bird in her
house I do not know!" she said. "Ben did warn

Urk that he was a real menace, into every kind of
mischief, and I can see he didn't exaggerate. Six
patties and seventy-five-pee's worth of blackcurrant
ice! You take him straight back to the house, Arabel
Jones, and put him in the meat-safe, and there he
stays, till Ben and Martha come to fetch you."

The various customers sitting at the little red
plastic tables were greatly interested in all this
excitement, and many heads turned to look at
Mortimer, who had ended up jammed head-first
in the knife-and-fork rack at the end of the counter,
and was now yelling loudly to be released.

Luckily it turned out that Lord Donisthorpe
was very fond of cream-cheese patties with blackcurrant ice-cream.

"Here," he said, handing Arabel the red and
yellow ice-cream cones, which he had been
holding. "You take these while I find some more
money. There you are, Mrs Jones, this will pay
for the damaged patties and all the ice-cream with
which they came in contact; pray put them all on
a large plate, and then I will eat them, which will
save me having to boil myself an egg later. Now
– if I just remove the raven from the knife-rack –
I do not believe that any more need be said

about this matter."

Aunt Effie looked as if she violently disagreed, but since Lord Donisthorpe was the owner of the zoo she was obliged to give way. Mortimer was much too busy to trouble his head about the furious glances Aunt Effie was giving him; released from the knife-rack, he sat on the red plastic table between Arabel and Lord Donisthorpe, holding his dandelion ice-cream cone in his claw and studying it admiringly. Then he ate it very fast in one bite and two swallows – crunch, hoosh, swallop – and then he looked round to see what everybody else was doing. Arabel had mostly finished her quince ice-cream – which was delicious – but Lord Donisthorpe still had quite a number of cream-cheese patties to go, so Mortimer helped him with four of them.

Meanwhile, at a table by the window, two men, one of them wearing a hat and one not, had been watching this scene, and were now staring thought-fully at Mortimer.

The hatless man took his teacup and went back to the counter to have it refilled. "That seems to be a very badly-behaved bird," he said to Aunt Effie, as she handed him his cup and he gave her the money.

"You can say that again," snapped Aunt Effie. "He has to stay in my house while my brother-in-law has his veryclose veins operated on, but I certainly intend to see he does as little damage as possible while he's here. The havoc that Monster has wreaked at my brother-in-law's you'd never credit – eaten whole gas-stoves and kitchen sinks, he has – worse than a tribe of Tartar Sorcerers, he is! Into the meat-safe he goes the minute he gets back to my house, I can tell you."

"A very sensible plan, madam," the hatless man agreed. "And if I were you, I should put that meat-safe out-of-doors. A bird like that can harbour all sorts of infection – it would be downright danger-ous to have it in the house."

"That's true," said Aunt Effie. "We could all come down with Raven Delirium, or get Inter-city-cosis from him. I'll put the meat-safe out on the front lawn. And if it rains, so much the better; I don't suppose that black Fiend ever had a wash in his life."

The hatless man went back to the window-table with his tea. While he was waiting for it to cool, he said to his friend in a low voice, "We can pin the blame on the bird. All we have to do is to open the meat-safe. Everybody will think that *he* let out the animals."

Presently the two men left the cafeteria and strolled away, glancing carelessly at the giraffe-house, the zebra-bower, and the ostrich-haven as they passed. Then they left the zoo.

Arabel thanked Lord Donisthorpe for her and Mortimer's treats. Lord Donisthorpe patted her head and gave her a ten-penny piece. "That will buy your raven another doughnut," he said. "But I should wait till tomorrow."

"Oh yes, he's full up now," said Arabel.

Mortimer, absolutely stuffed with ice-cream and cheese patty, made no difficulty about going home to bed.

"I'll be back at the house in twenty minutes," called Aunt Effie from the counter, where she was washing up the used knives and forks. "Don't you let that bird touch *anything* in the house. Tell your Uncle Urk I said so."

Going towards home, Arabel and Mortimer caught up with Uncle Urk, whose jobs were finished and who was intending to watch television.

"Uncle Urk," said Arabel, "I think those two men who were in the cafeteria are animal thieves. They were in the same railway carriage with me and Mortimer, and they were talking about zebras and giraffes and ostriches."

"*Course* they were talking about zebras and giraffes and ostriches, Arabel dearie," said Uncle Urk kindly. "'Cos they was acoming to the zoo, see? Natural, people talks about zebras and camels and giraffes when they're a-going to *see* ostriches and giraffes and camels."

"I think they were thieves," said Arabel. "Don't you think so, Mortimer?"

"Kaaark," said Mortimer.

"Can't take what that bird says as evidence," said Uncle Urk. "'Sides, little gals gets to fancying things, *I* know. Little gals is very fanciful creatures. That's what you bin a-doing, Arabel dearie – you got to fancying things about animal thieves. We won't mention it to your Aunt Effie, eh, case she gets nervous? Terrible nervous your Aunt Effie can get, once she begins."

"But, Uncle Urk," said Arabel.

"Now, Arabel dearie, don't you trouble your head about such things – *or* mine," said Uncle Urk, who was dying to watch Rumbury Wanderers play Liverpool United, and he hurried into the house.

Chapter Three

Arabel saw that Chris, whose evening jobs were finished, had taken his guitar into Uncle Urk's garden. Arabel and Mortimer loved listening to Chris play, so they went and sat beside him and he sang:

> *"Arabel's raven is quick on the draw,*
> *Better steer clear of his beak and his claw,*
> *When there is trouble, you know in your bones,*
> *Right in the middle is Mortimer Jones!"*

Mortimer drew himself up and looked immensely proud that a song had been written about him. Arabel sucked her finger and leaned against an apple tree.

Inside the house, Uncle Urk suddenly thought: What if Arabel was right about those men being giraffe thieves? Ben says she's mostly a sensible little thing. I'd look silly if she'd a-warned me, and I didn't do anything, and they really *was* thieves.

42

So, after thinking about it for a while, he rang up Sam Heyward, the night-watchman, on the zoo internal telephone. "Sam," he said, "I got a kind of a feeling there might be a bit o' trouble tonight, so why don't you let old Noah loose? It's months since he had a night out. You never know, if there's any miscreants abouts, he might put a spoke in their wheel."

"O.K. Urk, if you say so," said Sam. "Anyways, old Noah might catch a few rabbits; there's a sight too many rabbits about in the park just now, eating up all the wildebeest food."

Sam left his night-watchman's hut to let out Noah the boa, who was very pleased to have the freedom of the park again, and slithered quietly away through the grass. When Sam returned to his hut, he didn't notice that a small tube had been slipped under the door, in the crack at the hinge end. As soon as he shut the door a sweet-smelling gas began to dribble in through the tube. By slow degrees Sam became drowsier and drowsier, until, after about half an hour, he toppled right off his stool and lay on the matting fast asleep, dreaming that he had put ten pounds on a horse in the Derby called Horseradish, and that it had been on the

point of winning when Noah the boa, who
could travel at a terrific speed when he chose to,
suddenly shot under the tape just ahead of
Horseradish, and won the race.

Meanwhile, in Uncle Urk's garden, Chris sang,

"Arabel's raven is perfectly hollow,
What he can't chew up he'll manage to swallow –
Furniture – fire-escapes – fencing – and phones –
All are digested by Mortimer Jones."

Mortimer looked even prouder.
Chris sang,

"When the ice-cream disappears from the cones,
When you are deafened by shrieks or by moans,
When the fur's flying, or the air's full of stones,
You can be certain –"

Just at this moment Aunt Effie came home. As
soon as she was through the gate, she said: "Chris!
Fetch out that meat-safe!"

Looking rather startled, Chris laid down his
guitar and did as he was told. He placed the meat-
safe under the apple-tree.

Instantly, Aunt Effie grabbed Mortimer, thrust
him into the safe (which he completely filled), shut

the door, and slammed home the catch.

A fearful cry came from inside.

"There!" said Aunt Effie. "Now, you go up
to bed, Arabel Jones, and I don't want to hear a
single sound out of you, or out of that bird, till
morning – do you hear me?"

Since Mortimer, inside the meat-safe, was
making a noise like a troop of roller-skaters crossing a tin bridge, and shouting "Nevermore!" at
the top of his lungs, it was quite hard for Arabel
to hear what Aunt Effie said, but she could easily
understand what her aunt meant.

Arabel went quietly and sadly up to bed, but she had not the least intention of leaving Mortimer to pass the night inside the meat-safe. He hasn't done anything bad in Aunt Effie's house, Arabel thought. So why should he be punished by being shut inside the meat-safe? It isn't fair. Besides, Mortimer can't *stand* being shut up.

Indeed, the noise from the meat-safe could be heard for two hundred yards around Uncle Urk's house. But Aunt Effie went indoors and turned up the volume of the television very loud, in order to drown Mortimer's yells and bangs.

"When he learns who's master he'll soon settle down," she said grimly.

Arabel always did exactly as she was told. Aunt Effie had said, "I don't want to hear a single sound out of you," so, as soon as it was dark, and Aunt Effie and Uncle Urk had gone to bed, Arabel put on her dressing-gown and slippers and went very softly down the stairs and out through the front door, which she had to unlock. She did not make a single sound.

Mortimer had quieted down, just a little, inside the meat-safe, but he was very far from asleep. He was making a miserable mumbling groaning to himself, and kicking and scratching with his claws. Arabel softly undid the catch.

"Hush, Mortimer!" she whispered. "We don't want to wake them."

They could hear Uncle Urk's snores coming out through the bedroom window. The sound was like somebody grinding a bunch of rusty wires along a section of corrugated iron, ending with a tremendous rattle.

Mortimer was so glad to see Arabel that he went quite silent. She lifted him out of the meat-safe and held him tight, flattening his feathers, which were all endways and ruffled. Then she carried him back up the stairs to her bedroom.

Mortimer did not usually like sleeping on a bed; he preferred a bread-bin or a coal-scuttle or the airing-cupboard; but he had been so horrified by the meat-safe that he was happy to share Arabel's eiderdown, though he did peck a hole in it so that most of the feathers came out. Either because of all the feathers flying around, or because of the excitements of the day, neither Arabel nor Mortimer slept very well.

Mortimer was dreaming about giraffes. Arabel was dreaming about Noah the boa.

After an hour or so, Mortimer suddenly shot bolt upright in bed.

"What is it, Mortimer?" whispered Arabel. She knew that Mortimer's ears were very keen, like those of an owl; he could hear a potato crisp fall on to a carpeted floor half a mile away.

Mortimer turned his head, intently listening. Now even Arabel thought she could hear something, past Uncle Urk's snores a soft series of muffled thumps.

"Oh, my goodness, Mortimer! Do you think those men are stealing Lord Donisthorpe's giraffes?"

Mortimer did think so. His boot-button black eyes gleamed with pleasure at the thought. Arabel could see this because the moon was shining brightly through the window.

"I had better wake up Uncle Urk," said Arabel. "Though Aunt Effie will be cross, because she said she didn't want to hear me."

She went and tapped on Uncle Urk's door and said in a soft polite voice, so as not to disturb Aunt Effie: "Uncle Urk. Would you come out, please? We believe that thieves are stealing your giraffes."

But the noise made by Uncle Urk as he snored was so tremendous that neither he nor Aunt Effie (who was snoring a bit on her own account) could possibly hear Arabel's polite tones.

"Oh dear, Mortimer," said Arabel then. "I wonder what we had better do."

Mortimer plainly thought that they ought to let well alone. His expression suggested that if every giraffe in the zoo were hijacked he, personally, would not raise any objection.

"Perhaps we could wake up Lord Donisthorpe," Arabel said, and she went downstairs and into the garden, with Mortimer sitting on her shoulder.

But when they were close to it, Lord Donisthorpe's castle looked very difficult to enter. There was a moat, and a drawbridge, which was raised, and a massive wooden door, which was shut.

Then Arabel remembered that Chris slept in a wooden hut near the ostrich enclosure.

"We'll wake Chris," she told Mortimer. "He'll know what to do."

Mortimer was greatly enjoying the trip through the moonlit zoo. He did not mind where they went, or what they did, so long as they did not go back to bed too soon.

Arabel walked quietly over the grass in her bedroom slippers. "Chris sleeps in the hut with red geraniums in the window-boxes," she said. "He showed it to me while the doughnuts were cooking."

"Kaaark," said Mortimer, thinking about doughnuts.

Arabel walked up to the hut with the red geraniums and banged on the door.

"Chris!" she called softly. "It's me – Arabel! Will you open the door, please?"

It took a long time to wake Chris. Nobody had pumped any gas under his door; he was just naturally a very heavy sleeper. But at last he woke and came stumbling and yawning to open the door. He was very surprised to see Arabel.

"Arabel! And Mortimer! What ever are you

doing up at this time of night? Your Aunt Effie
would blow her top!"

"Ssssh!" said Arabel. "Chris, Mortimer and I
think there are thieves in the zoo. Can't you hear
a kind of thumping and bumping, coming from
the zebra house?"

Chris listened and thought he could. "I'd best
set off the alarm," he said. "Lord Donisthorpe

always tells us, better ten false alarms than lose one animal."

He pressed the alarm button, which ought to have let off tremendously loud sirens at different points all over the park. But nothing happened.

"That's funny," Chris said, scratching his head and yawning some more. Then his eyes and his mouth opened wide, and he said: "Blimey! It *must* be thieves. They must have cut the wire. I'd best go on my bike and rouse Lord Donisthorpe, I know a back way into the castle, and then he can phone the police. *You'd* better stop here, Arabel, until I get back; you shouldn't be running about the zoo in your slippers if there's thieves around."

Chris started off on his bike towards Lord Donisthorpe's castle. Arabel would have stayed in his hut, as he asked her, but Mortimer had other ideas. He hoisted himself off Arabel's shoulder and began flapping heavily along the ground in the direction of the giraffe house.

"Mortimer !" called Arabel. " Come back!"

But Mortimer took no notice, and so Arabel started in pursuit of him.

To Arabel's horror, as she went after Mortimer, she saw a truck parked outside the zebra house.

Men with black bowler hats crammed so far down over their heads that their faces were invisible, stood by the truck packing in limp zebras, which seemed to be fast asleep.

"Oh, how awful!" said Arabel. "Mortimer, stop! The thieves are stealing the zebras!"

But Mortimer was not interested in zebra thieves. He had only one idea in his head and that was to get to the doughnut machine near the giraffe house. The thieves did not notice Arabel and Mortimer pass by, and Arabel caught up with Mortimer just as he perched on the machine.

"Kaaark!" he said, giving the machine a hopeful kick.

"If I get you a doughnut, Mortimer, will you come back with me quietly to Chris's hut?" said Arabel. She had the ten-penny piece that Lord Donisthorpe had given her in her dressing-gown pocket.

Mortimer made no answer, but jumped up and down on top of the machine.

So Arabel put her coin in the slot, and Mortimer, almost standing on his head with interest and enthusiasm, watched the doughnut slide down into the oil to cook; then he watched

the hook hoist it out and the puffer blow white crystals all over it; then he watched it tumble out into the paper cup; then he grabbed it, jumped down off the machine, and disappeared in the direction of the giraffe-house.

"Mortimer, come back!" called Arabel. "You promised! –"

But that was all she said, for next minute she found herself wrapped up as tightly as if twenty yards of oil pipeline had been wound round her, and she found herself staring, stiff with fright, straight into the thoughtful face of Noah the boa.

Chapter Four

Meanwhile the thieves, working at top speed,
had packed all the drugged zebras into their truck,
with layers of foam rubber in between. Then they
went on to the ostriches. It was easy to drug the
ostriches; all they needed to do was sprinkle
chloroform on the sand where the ostriches hid
their heads, and then make an alarming noise; in
five minutes all the ostriches were out flat.

"D'you reckon we've time to take in a few
camels as well as the giraffes?" asked Fred the
truck-driver, when the ostriches were packed in.
"Camels are fetching very fancy prices just now,
up Blackpool way."

But the short fat man was looking towards
Lord Donisthorpe's castle, where a light had come
on in one of the windows, high up.

"That looks like trouble," he said.

"Maybe the old geezer heard something. We

better not fool around; go straight for the giraffes, get them packed in, and get away."

At this moment, Lord Donisthorpe was speaking on the phone to the local police. "Yes, Inspector; as I just told you, we have reason to believe that there are thieves on my estate, engaged in stealing animals – *who* told me so?

I understand that a raven, of unusually acute hearing, informed a young person named Arabel Jones, who informed a youthful attendant at the zoo – who informed *me* –"

At this moment also, Noah the boa, who had decided, after careful inspection of Arabel, that she looked as if she might be good to eat, probably not *quite* as good as a doughnut, but still much better than a rabbit, had thrown an extra loop of himself round both Arabel and the doughnut machine, to which he was hitched, and had begun to squeeze, at the same time opening his mouth wider and wider.

But his squeezing had an unexpected effect. It started the doughnut machine working, just as if somebody had put in a coin.

Arabel, doing her best to keep quite calm, said politely, "Excuse me: but if you wouldn't mind undoing the coil that is holding my hands, *here*, I would be able to press the lever and then I could get you a doughnut, if you'd like?"

Noah was not very bright, but he did understand the word *doughnut*, and Arabel's wriggling of her hands indicated what she meant. He loosened one of his coils; Arabel pressed the lever twice; and the machine, ever so quickly, sugared a doughnut and tossed it out into a paper cup. Noah swallowed it in a flash, and, as the machine was still working, Arabel pressed the lever again.

Meanwhile the thieves had quietly moved their truck on to the giraffe-house, parked, and gone inside.

"*Blimey*," said Fred, "what, in the name of all

that's 'orrible, 'as been going on 'ere?"

For when they shone their flashlights around, a scene of perfectly hopeless confusion was revealed: all that could be seen was legs of giraffes at the bottom of the spiral stair, while their necks, like some dreadfully tangled piece of knitting, were all twined up inside the spiral.

"Strewth!" said the short fat man. "How are we *ever* going to get them out of there?"

Meanwhile Lord Donisthorpe and Chris, both riding bicycles, were dashing through the zoo, hunting for the malefactors. Chris was dreadfully worried about Arabel, because he had found his hut empty; he kept calling, as he rode along, "Arabel? Mortimer? Where are you?"

At this moment the thieves, feverishly trying to untangle the necks of the giraffes and drag them out of the spiral stair, heard the unmistakable gulping howl of a police-car siren, coming fast.

"Here, we better scarper," said the fat man.

"They got cops in helicopters?" said Fred. "The sound o' that siren seems to be coming from dead overhead."

"It's the acoustics of this building, thickhead."

"Never mind where the perishing sound's

coming from," said the pale man. "We better hop it. At least we've got the ostriches and the zebras."

They ran for their truck. But Chris, who reached it just before them, had taken the key out of the ignition. The thieves were obliged to abandon their van and escape on foot. And as they pounded towards the distant gate, something like a main drain travelling at thirty miles an hour caught up with them, flung a half-hitch round each of them, and brought them to the ground.

It was Noah who, having, for once in his life, eaten as many doughnuts as he wanted, was now prepared to do his job of burglar-catching.

Chris went in search of Arabel and found her, rather pale and faint, sitting by the doughnut machine. Mortimer, looking very pleased with himself indeed, was perched on her shoulder, still giving his celebrated imitation of a police-car siren.

When the real police turned up, half an hour later, all they had to do was take the thieves off to jail. Then, greatly to Arabel's relief, Lord Donisthorpe took Noah back to his cage, wheeling him in a barrow.

Chris and Lord Donisthorpe had already unpacked the ostriches and zebras and laid them out in the fresh air to sleep off the effects of the drug they had been given.

But it took ever so much longer to untangle the giraffes from the spiral stair. In fact they were obliged to dismantle the top part of the stair altogether.

"I can't think how they ever *got* their necks in like this," said Lord Donisthorpe, panting. "Let alone *why*."

Chris thought he could guess. He had found traces of doughnut on each step all the way up.

"Perhaps it's not such a good plan to have a spiral stair in the giraffe-house," murmured Lord

Donisthorpe, as the last captive – Wendy – was carefully pulled out, set upright on her spindly legs, and given a pail of giraffe-food to revive her.

"Well, I certainly am greatly obliged to you three," added Lord Donisthorpe to Arabel and Chris, who had helped to extract Wendy, and to Mortimer, who had been sitting on the stair-rail and enjoying the spectacle. "But for you, my zoo would have suffered severe losses tonight, and I hope I can do something for you in return."

Chris said politely that he didn't think he wanted anything. He just liked working in the zoo.

Mortimer didn't even bother to reply. He was remembering how enjoyable it had been to entice Wendy, Elsie, and Derek farther and farther up the spiral stair by holding the doughnut just in front of their noses.

But Arabel said, "Oh, please, Lord Donisthorpe. Could you please ask Aunt Effie *not* to shut Mortimer up in the meat-safe? He does hate it so."

"Perhaps it would be best," said Lord Donisthorpe thoughtfully, "if Mortimer came to stay with me in my castle while you remain at Foxwell. I believe ravens are often to be found in castles.

And there is really very little harm he can do there. If any."

"Oh, *yes*," said Arabel. "He'd *love* to live in a castle, wouldn't you, Mortimer?"

"Kaaark," said Mortimer.

And so that is what happened.

Aunt Effie and Uncle Urk were quite astonished when they woke up next morning and learned all that had been going on during the night. But Aunt Effie was not able to scold Arabel or Mortimer, as Lord Donisthorpe said they had been the means of saving all his ostriches and zebras, not to mention the giraffes.

Arabel soon became very fond of Wendy, Derek, and Elsie; though she had continual trouble preventing Mortimer from teasing them.

But she never did get to like Noah the boa.

ARABEL AND MORTIMER

Have you read these other
books in the series?

Arabel's Raven
978-1-84780-691-8

Arabel, Mortimer and the Escaped Black Mamba
978-1-84780-693-2

Mortimer and the Sword Excalibur
978-1-84780-692-5